To Camden and Calum,
two of my favorite little boys

Farrar Straus Giroux Books for Young Readers
An imprint of Macmillan Publishing Group, LLC
175 Fifth Avenue, New York 10010

Text and illustrations copyright © 2017 by Amy Young
All rights reserved
Color separations by Bright Arts (H.K.) Ltd.
Printed in China by Toppan Leefung Printing Ltd.,
Dongguan City, Guangdong Province
Designed by Kristie Radwilowicz
First edition, 2017
1 3 5 7 9 10 8 6 4 2

mackids.com

Library of Congress Cataloging-in-Publication Data

Names: Young, Amy, author, illustrator.
Title: A new friend for Sparkle / Amy Young.
Description: First edition. | New York : Farrar Straus Giroux, [2017] |
    Summary: When Lucy's friend Brock visits, Sparkle the "unicorn" is jealous until he and
    Brock discover a shared love of drumming and dancing.
Identifiers: LCCN 2016038110 | ISBN 9780374305536 (hardcover)
Subjects: | CYAC: Friendship—Fiction. | Jealousy—Fiction. | Unicorns—Fiction. |
    Goats—Fiction.
Classification: LCC PZ7.Y845 New 2017 | DDC [E]—dc23
LC record available at https://lccn.loc.gov/2016038110

Our books may be purchased in bulk for promotional, educational, or business use. Please
contact your local bookseller or the Macmillan Corporate and Premium Sales Department at
(800) 221-7945 ext. 5442 or by e-mail at MacmillanSpecialMarkets@macmillan.com.

A New Friend for SPARKLE

Amy Young

FARRAR STRAUS GIROUX
NEW YORK

Lucy put food in Sparkle's bowl. She said, "My friend Cole is coming over today. You'll like him. He is a lot of fun.

"I don't think he has ever met a unicorn before."

When Cole got there, he said, "Hi, Lucy. What a cool goat! What's his name?"

Lucy said, "He is not a goat. He is a unicorn, and his name is Sparkle."

"Oh, sorry, Sparkle."

"Lucy, look what I brought!"

"Yay! And here are my toys."

Lucy and Cole

started

to play.

They forgot that Sparkle
was even there.

He had to remind them.

"Sparkle! What are you doing?"

"**HEY!**" said Lucy.
"You ruined my ball!"

"You go sit over there until you can play nicely!"

Sparkle sat and moped.

Lucy and Cole played some more.
Then Cole took out his drum.

BANG!

BANG! BANG!

BANG!

Sparkle perked up his ears.

He liked that sound!

Sparkle inched toward Cole and the drum.

"Does Sparkle want to play my drum?"

Lucy said, "I don't think he knows how."

But Sparkle tap-tap-tapped on the
drum with his horn.

tap

tap

tap

tap

Cole played some more. "Sparkle, can you dance?"

Lucy said, "I'm pretty
sure that unicorns
don't dance."

But Sparkle was dancing and jumping like it was the most fun he'd ever had.

Lucy said, "I'm tired of this."

They kept right on
dancing and banging.

Lucy yelled,

"STOP THAT RIGHT NOW!"

Everyone got very still.

Then Sparkle picked up the drum
and carefully brought it to Lucy.

"I don't know how to play the drum," said Lucy.

"It's easy. You just hit it, like this," said Cole, and
he showed her.

"Hmph," said Lucy. She tried it.

"That's the idea," said Cole.

She tried it again.

Sparkle shook his butt to the beat.

BANG!

BANG!

BANG!

BANG!

They all took turns dancing and banging on the drum,

until they were tired out.

Finally, it was time for Cole to go home.

"Sparkle, you are one cool unicorn," said Cole.

Sparkle nuzzled Cole and
gave him a big, wet lick.

Later, Lucy and Sparkle shared a cupcake.

"Cole is a good friend, isn't he?" Lucy said.

Sparkle nodded.

"But you are my very best friend."